LEGACY OF THE BLADE

SERIES PREQUEL

ELIZABETH ROSE

ROSESCRIBE MEDIA INC.

Cover created by Elizabeth Rose Krejcik
Edited by Scott Moreland

ISBN-13: 978-1727854473
ISBN-10: 1727854470

CHAPTER 1

Seven-year-old Corbett Blake held tightly to the hand of his three-year-old sister, Wren, as they watched their grandfather's body, the late Lord Frederick of Steepleton, being lowered into the ground.

Their father, Lord Evan Blake, walked forward and threw the first shovel of dirt over the deceased man. Frederick was Evan's late father and had also been Lord of Blake Castle.

Corbett's mother, Lady Eleanor, walked up next, taking the shovel from her husband and only lifted a small amount of dirt since she was very pregnant and about to give birth any day now. She was carrying twins, or so the old sorcerer had told them. He'd foreseen it in his gazing crystal.

Corbett's mother then turned around and tried to

hand the shovel to him, her bright, blue eyes consoling him as she did so. His mother was a vision of beauty with her long, dark hair braided and twisted around each ear. Her head remained covered with a light, transparent veil.

He hesitated, his eyes scanning the grounds of the church graveyard, seeing the huge crowd staring at him now. Corbett's uncle, Brother Ruford, smiled at him and nodded his tonsured head. His hands remained folded in prayer and hidden beneath the folds of his coarsely-woven, black robe.

"Go ahead," came his father's voice from behind him, reaching out and taking the shovel from his wife and placing it into Corbett's small hands. "You are of fostering age now, Son, and, hopefully, someday will follow in your grandfather's footsteps. You need to show your respect."

Corbett gingerly took the shovel, never having done this before. He moved forward cautiously, stopping at the edge of the hole in the ground. His grandfather's wooden casket stared up at him. Just the sight of it had Corbett's stomach clenching in a vast array of emotions. He knew what a fierce warrior Frederick Blake had been, losing his life in battle protecting King Edward III. He also knew his father had been in that battle and was the reason Frederick's dead body was brought from the field and not left for the ravens to peck out his eyes.

A raven landed on the wooden cross serving as a grave marker, letting out a squawk and causing Corbett to jump. Then the bird headed back up into the sky. It startled him to be thinking about ravens and then have one appear out of nowhere. Ravens were an eerie type of bird that Corbett was sure came directly from hell.

He glanced over to see his mother rubbing her large belly and comforting his sister, Wren. Wren's long, dark hair fanned out around her and her eyes focused on him. She let go of her mother's hand and ran over to join him.

"I'll help you, Corby," she said bravely, being much too young to be of any use in lifting a shovel of dirt. She adored Corbett and would do anything for her big brother.

"No, Wren, go back to Mother," he told her, sending her on her way. Standing off from the gravesite, he saw not only his father and uncle, but also the old sorcerer, Orrick, conversing softly and looking in his direction.

He turned around again, thinking of the dream he'd had a sennight ago that warned him that his grandfather would die. He'd seen this exact scene in his head. By dropping dirt atop the dead man, he'd be more or less sealing his fate as some kind of seer, or having some sort of special powers. He didn't want that. Magic was something he didn't really believe in. Now, he regretted ever having told Orrick, since the mystical man was a good friend of Corbett's father.

He shoveled the dirt atop the casket quickly, turning around only to have the sorcerer take the shovel from him next.

"You are special, Corbett," the old man told him. "You know things. You have dreams." Orrick was a tall man with a weathered face and mysterious eyes that seemed to change from blue to green and even to amethyst at times. He had long, white hair and a beard and mustache. He wore a long, purple cape over a dark tunic and hose. The cape flowed out behind him when he walked, making the man seem ethereal.

"Nay, it was naught but a silly dream, that's all." Corbett looked back up to his father who was watching them intently with a look of sadness upon his face. His father was a handsome man with regal features and dark hair. Lord Evan Blake always made sure to look his best. Even after a battle, he would change into fresh clothes and clean his wounds quickly, not liking to been seen looking less than perfect.

"I have spoken to your father about having you live with me back in Torquay. I'd like to see what else you have the capability of doing."

Corbett's eyes darted across the graveyard to Kenric, the Baron of Torquay. The baron's wife, Gilda, was back in Torquay and pregnant as well. Corbett had seen her once when he'd gone to visit his father and decided immediately that he didn't like her. She unsettled him for some reason that he couldn't explain.

Corbett didn't want to live in Torquay. But since his father lived there, acting as the baron's captain of the guard, Corbett figured it wouldn't be so bad. At least he'd be living with his father, once again. He only wished his mother and sister could be there, too. But for some reason, the baroness didn't want them there. So, they'd stayed in Steepleton and lived with Corbett's grandfather instead. Corbett longed for the day when they'd all live together as one, big, happy family again.

"Corbett," called his father. Corbett's eyes darted up to see his father speaking with the baron now. "Come here, Son." His father waved him over. The look of sadness he'd seen on his father's face was gone, and it was replaced by one of pride and contentment.

"Go to him," said Orrick, urging the boy forward.

Corbett did as he was told, joining the two men.

"What is it, Father?" he asked, already experiencing a new knot forming in his stomach. He had a feeling that whatever his father said next was not going to be to his liking.

"Corbett. Son," said his father, putting his hand on Corbett's shoulder. "The baron has just declared me the new Lord of Steepleton. I'll hold the title and also the lands your grandfather once held."

Corbett's heart sank at hearing this news. He needed to act happy for his father's sake and out of respect, but this meant his father would be living in Steepleton now, just when Corbett was being sent to live in Torquay.

"But . . . what will happen to me?" asked Corbett.

"Orrick will be watching over you now," his father told him. "He says he thinks you have a special gift. You might even have the chance of becoming his apprentice."

"Apprentice?" This was horrible news. Corbett wanted to follow in his grandfather and father's footsteps. He'd dreamed of being a warrior and fighting at his father's side. This couldn't be happening. This was awful. This would not only take him away from his entire family, but also far from his hopes and dreams of someday becoming a knight or, perhaps, lord of his own castle.

"Don't sound so horrified," his father told him with a chuckle. "I know it's not what we planned, but everything happens for a reason. Perhaps you, just like my brother, Ruford, are not meant to be warriors. The fates must have something else planned for you, Corbett."

"But . . . I'm your only son," he pleaded. "I'm your

oldest child. I should be a knight like you, someday. Shouldn't I?"

"Your father will have more sons," said the baron, trying to comfort him but only making him feel worse. "Your mother is pregnant with twins I hear. For all we know they could both be boys. Your father might have several sons to foster in the ways of a warrior, after all."

"Why can't I stay here?" asked Corbett. "Orrick has chambers here as well. Can't I train with him at Blake Castle instead?"

"Nay," answered his father with a shake of his head. "Orrick thinks it will be too distracting being around your mother and siblings. It would be best for you to concentrate on your studies away from your family and Blake Castle."

"No," said Corbett, shaking his head. "Father, this isn't the way it is supposed to be."

"Have you had another vision?" asked Orrick, anxiously coming to his side. "Perhaps you've seen something in the future we should know about?" Orrick touched the crystal orb hanging on a cord from around his neck.

Corbett fingered the baby ring with the Blake crest of an eagle hanging from a chain around his neck. This was the ring his father had given him the day he was born. His sister, Wren, had one also. His father was preparing to give the new babies rings, too.

Corbett toyed with the idea of telling them he'd had a dream that he was supposed to be a knight, not a sorcerer's apprentice. If he said that, then mayhap they'd change their minds and keep him at Blake Castle with his family after all. Or, at least, it might give him the opportunity of being fostered out as a page instead of some sort of apprentice to magic and things he didn't understand. Yes, this could be the answer to all his problems, but he knew in his heart he couldn't lie to his father.

"Nay, I had no dream," he said with a downward glance and a shake of his head. His admittance was the nail in his own coffin, as he now feared his fate of possibly never seeing his family again.

CHAPTER 2

*T*wo days later, Corbett stood in the courtyard of Blake Castle at the sorcerer's side. His trunk was packed and already put upon the cart they'd use to travel to his new home in Torquay. It was late in the day, and nightfall would be setting in soon. Orrick told him they would travel by moonlight, as a full moon would guide their way and make their powers stronger. Several guards would be accompanying them on the trip for added protection.

Corbett's family was all there to see him off. He hugged and kissed his mother, then did the same to his young sister, Wren.

"Be strong, Corbett." His father gave him a hug next.

"I'll miss you, Father," Corbett told him with a heavy heart.

"You can come and visit us any time you'd like."

"That's right," said his mother, stepping forward, rubbing her belly and breathing heavier than she ever had before. "Once the babies are born, you can come back and see them, too."

Corbett turned and walked silently to the cart at Orrick's side. Hearing a shout from his sister, he spun around to see her dashing across the cobbled stones and heading right for him.

"Corby, don't leave!" Wren shot forward, only to crash into an old man with a walking staff who was blind. Corbett's father rushed over and picked up the girl and put her on her feet. Then he reached into his pouch and pulled out a coin and pressed it into the blind man's hand.

"Why are you giving a coin to that blind beggar?" asked Corbett.

"Just because he's blind doesn't mean he doesn't deserve a coin or a kind word," his father explained. "Remember that, both of you." He looked first to Wren and then over to Corbett. "Blindness might be the lack of sight, but I believe the blind have an inner sight they use instead."

"Aye, Father, I will remember that," said Corbett. His little sister ran to him once again, crying and wrapping her arms around his leg, not wanting him to leave.

He bent down and helped her to her feet, knowing he had to be the strong one now. "It'll be all right, Wren," he told her, giving her a quick hug. "Now, go back to mother."

Wren wiped the tears from her eyes and did as Corbett told her. Corbett heard a slight sigh from Orrick and turned to see him shaking his head.

"What's the matter, Orrick?" he asked.

"It's an omen. A bad omen," the sorcerer mumbled softly so only Corbett could hear him.

"What is?"

"Your sister, Wren, crashed into that blind man and fell. It is not a good sign for what is coming in her future, I am afraid."

Corbett wanted to scream out that it wasn't true. But unfortunately, he'd had a slight ill feeling for his sister as well when she'd crashed into the blind man. He couldn't deny what he'd felt. Still, he refused to believe anything bad would ever happen to his dear, younger sister.

A rider came through the gates at a good clip and the herald blew a loud note on the straight trumpet, announcing a visitor.

"Who is it?" asked Corbett, seeing his father as well as the baron rush forward to greet the man.

"He wears the king's crest," Orrick pointed out. "He must be the king's messenger."

"What is he doing here?"

"I'm not sure, but I do know the king was passing through close by here recently. It must be of importance since the man rides so quickly and arrives so late in the day. Let's go find out, shall we?"

Corbett followed the sorcerer over to the small group of men.

"Baron Torquay, the king sends me with this missive," said the man, dismounting and holding out the parchment sealed with wax and the stamp of the king's signet ring.

"What is it?" asked Evan, looking at the baron – his liege lord, as the man read the words upon the parchment.

"It seems the king has heard that I've given lordship of Blake Castle to you already," said the baron, continuing to read.

"How could he know that already?" asked Evan.

"The king has heard it from a peddler who came from Blake Castle," the messenger informed him.

"Evan, I am sorry, but King Edward refuses to let me give Blake Castle and its lands to you." The baron threw the missive to the ground in disgust.

"Why?" asked Corbett's father.

Corbett bent down and picked up the parchment and attempted to read it.

"He knows you married the illegitimate daughter of the vicar instead of a titled woman. He says you have sullied the Blake name. He also wants to strip you of your title of not only lord but knight as well." The baron's face showed that he was not happy with the king's decision.

"What?" asked Corbett out loud. "Father, he can't do that!"

"Aye, he can, Son," said Evan with disappointment in his voice. "I hoped it would never come to this but, unfortunately, it has."

"What will happen to us now?" asked Corbett's mother coming forward with Wren at her side.

"I'll talk to the king," said the baron. "Perhaps I can change his mind."

"Oh, could you?" asked Corbett's mother with hope in her eyes.

The trumpet sounded again and a second rider made his way over the drawbridge and across the courtyard, dismounting so quickly that his horse hadn't even had a chance to stop.

"Another of the king's messengers," said Corbett softly, knowing this could not be a good thing.

"Baron," the man said, running to him with a missive in his hand, not waiting for the message to be read, but rather relaying it by mouth. "The king requests your presence. He also requests as many men as you can send, as thieves have been looting the harbor towns of the west coast."

"Oh!" shouted Corbett's mother, doubling over in pain and holding her belly.

"What's the matter?" asked Evan.

"It's . . . the babies," she cried out.

"He also says a pirate ship has been spotted and we need to ready ourselves for a possible sea attack," continued the messenger.

"Ow!" moaned Corbett's mother, bending over further this time, with both hands on her stomach.

"We'll go anon," said the baron. "Evan, you'll be at my side. We'll show the king your loyalty and I'll do all I can to change his decision."

"Why are thieves and pirates attacking the coast of Devon?" asked Evan. "They normally invade the channel on the east coast instead. I don't understand."

"They probably know they have a better chance of attack here, where the Cinque Ports ships aren't patrolling," said the baron. "Gather your men, Lord Blake, and meet me at the front gates."

"Right away, m'lord," said Evan, turning to go. Orrick took the missive from Corbett's hand and walked away, reading it.

"Father!" Corbett called out, stopping his father in

his tracks.

Corbett's mother was still bent over in pain. Corbett's eyes wandered over to her.

"Eleanor, are you really going to birth the babies now?" asked Evan.

"I can't help it," she said. "Yes, it is going to happen now."

"Then take these rings for the babies," said Evan, pulling two baby rings with yarn tied to them and handing them to his wife. "Handmaid," he called out to his wife's lady-in-waiting. "Take my wife to the solar quickly." He kissed his wife on the head and then did the same to his daughter, giving an instruction to a second handmaid. "You – watch over my daughter." Then he sent them away.

"I'm worried for Mother," said Corbett.

"Me, too," said Evan. "I only wish I didn't have to leave right now, Son, but I have no choice. I need to serve the king as well as try to save my title and lands from being taken from me."

"Please be safe," Corbett told him.

"I'll be safe." Evan pulled his sword from his scabbard and held it out in front of Corbett. "Do you see these four rings engraved upon my sword?"

"I do," said Corbett, reaching out to touch the interlocking circles just under the hilt.

"Each ring represents one of my children. Orrick put the etching on the sword and told me that my family will always be together and these interlocking rings symbolize it. This sword will be yours someday, Corbett."

"How could it be?" he asked, curiously. "I thought I was to be a sorcerer's apprentice, not a knight."

"You know I want you to be a knight even more than you want it, Son. Just keep the thought in your head and it'll happen someday." His father put his sword back into its sheath. "Now, I need you to go with Orrick until I return."

"I want to stay and look after Mother."

"She has handmaids and the midwife for that, now go."

"She needs more help. Please let me stay, Father."

"She'll have plenty of help, don't worry." He flagged down a woman in the shadows of the courtyard who was wearing a hooded robe and carrying two baskets covered with cloths. "You there, come here, anon."

"Me?" the plump woman looked up in surprise. Corbett couldn't see her face well, but noticed she was old.

"Aye, you. Go to the solar and help the handmaids in any way possible. My wife is giving birth and I am short on help at the moment."

"Of course, my lord," said the woman, looking more than happy. She bowed her head slightly and scurried away. As she left, Corbett saw her look back to a boy sitting atop a peddler's cart, nodding to him. Something didn't seem right.

"Father, I've never seen that woman before," said Corbett.

"She's probably one of the villagers and will know more about birthing babies than the handmaids. Now, go with Orrick. I have to gather the soldiers and leave to defend our king and lands."

As Evan Blake hurried away, Corbett realized his father did not know the people nor the soldiers of Blake Castle. He resided at the baron's side in Torquay and this was all new to him. However, Corbett knew the people well enough to realize the woman his father sent to the solar was not from the castle or the village. He had the awful feeling the woman could not be trusted.

"Let's go, Corbett," called the sorcerer from the bench atop the cart hitched to one old horse. Corbett couldn't disobey his father. He had to go with Orrick. But deep in his gut, he felt as if something was about to happen and it wasn't good.

Orrick spoke of omens when his sister knocked into the blind man. Well, Corbett was well aware of another omen. He'd seen his mother bend over and shout out with pain first when the messenger mentioned thieves, and then again when the man talked about pirates. Could this be some sort of omen related to the unborn babies? Thieves and pirates, he pondered the thought. He hoped this would have nothing to do with his new siblings at all.

"Corbett, get in the cart as we need to leave," instructed the sorcerer.

Corbett ran over and jumped onto the back of the cart as it lurched forward with a jerk, moving toward the drawbridge. His feet dangled over the back as they headed away.

He saw his father look up from a conversation with the soldiers and their eyes interlocked in a sad goodbye. His father smiled slightly and nodded his head and then tapped the hilt of his sword with his hand, reminding Corbett of their conversation. The sword would be his someday, his father had told him. That should make Corbett happy. But, for some reason, it only made him sad. He watched the castle getting smaller and smaller in the distance as they traveled to his new home. As the entourage of men headed out of the castle to protect their king and country, Corbett had the awful feeling that the sword was going to be his much sooner than either he or his father had ever imagined.

CHAPTER 3

*I*t had been nearly a sennight since Corbett had left Blake Castle, and there was still no word about his mother or the new babies. But then a messenger from Blake Castle came barreling into the courtyard one day, stopping his horse quickly and lowering himself to the ground. Rain pelted down around them like it'd been doing since the day they'd first started for Torquay. It was a bad omen in Corbett's mind. Lightning lit up the sky and thunder boomed in the distance.

"What is it?" asked Orrick, rushing over to the messenger boy. Corbett followed close behind.

"I have a missive from Brother Ruford," the lad told him.

"I'll take that," said the pregnant baroness, coming up

behind them and holding out her hand. Her handmaids followed, trying to hold a cloth held up with sticks over her head as she walked so she wouldn't get wet.

"I'm sorry, Baroness, but Brother Ruford told me to give the missive to Orrick directly." The messenger's eyes flitted from the baroness back over to Orrick, not sure what to do. He stood there looking confused, with the parchment in his hand and the water dripping down his face and arms.

"He said to give it to Orrick?" the baroness squawked. "A sorcerer? Stop being ridiculous and give it to me." She snatched the missive from the boy and tore it open, scanning the contents within. Then, with no emotion at all upon her face, she handed it to Orrick and threw her nose in the air never once even glancing at Corbett. "Here, this is of no concern to me."

She picked up her taffeta skirts now caked with mud and headed away. Her handmaidens followed along behind her, not doing much to keep her dry as she moved too fast for them to keep up. One of the women looked to be just as pregnant as the baroness and had a hard time lifting the cloth above the woman's head.

"What is it?" asked Corbett, watching the sorcerer scan the contents of the missive and then hand it to him.

"You know how to read, don't you?" Orrick asked.

"I've been learning," he said. "My uncle has been

teaching me." Corbett took the missive from Orrick. Rain ran down his arm and up his sleeve causing a cold shiver to spread through him. He looked at the parchment, able to make out enough of the words to know that it said something about his mother. He also saw the words babies and death, and couldn't read any more. "Tell me what it says," he said, pushing the missive back into Orrick's hand, not wanting to acknowledge that anything bad could have happened to his family.

"Your mother has had the babies," said Orrick.

"That's good news, then." Corbett tried to believe it, but he could feel a shadow covering the land.

"I'm sorry," said the messenger with a forlorn look upon his face. Orrick handed him a halfpenny for his trouble and the boy mounted his horse and headed away.

"Did the babies die in birth?" asked Corbett, waiting for Orrick's answer.

"Nay, Corbett, they didn't. But right afterward, they were stolen by a handmaid. It seems some of the guards went after her but she boarded a boat. With the storm we've been having, they think the boat capsized. The waters were rough and they couldn't go after them."

Corbett thought back to the woman who his father had sent to the solar to help his mother. She had to have been the one they were talking about. It was because of

Corbett's insistence that his mother needed more help that his father had even sent the woman in the first place. Now, Corbett felt awful. It was all his fault.

"There's more," said the sorcerer, putting his arm around Corbett and heading him out of the rain, back to the castle.

"Did something happen to Mother?" Corbett held his breath waiting for the man's answer.

"I'm sorry, lad, but it seems that she died giving birth."

"Nay!" Corbett shouted, not wanting to believe it. He tried to dart away, but Orrick pulled him back and held him against his purple robe. Corbett couldn't hold back his emotions. He broke down and cried. And when he heard the man's next words, he cried even harder.

"It seems that Wren has gone missing as well."

"This can't be. They have to find her."

"She was with a handmaiden who was bringing her here to you when they were attacked by bandits on the road. By the time the guard was able to fight them off, Wren disappeared into the forest. They tried to find her, but couldn't."

"Nay, this can't be happening," said Corbett, wiping a tear from his eye.

"As soon as your father gets back, I'm sure he'll send

out more search parties to look for her, Corbett. Don't worry about Wren."

"This can't be true," Corbett said, shaking his head in denial. "There is some mistake."

"It's no mistake," Orrick told him. "Now, come. Let's go to my chamber and I'll show you some of my potions. As soon as your father returns, things will be better, you'll see."

Corbett followed Orrick up to his tower chamber, hoping the man was right. His heart ached deeply for his mother and he wanted nothing more than to be with his sister right now to comfort her in this time of sorrow. Although he didn't even know if his newborn siblings were boys or girls, he missed them as well. His father would be devastated to hear the news when he returned, as his family meant everything to him.

Lord Evan Blake was different from most noblemen. Corbett had heard the wagging tongues of the alewives gossiping and saying that instead of marrying for alliances or wealth, his father married for love. Now, Corbett realized it was a decision that had cost his father dearly in the long run. Corbett could only hope the king would change his mind. When his father returned, he'd be landless and without a title all because he married for love. To make matters worse, he would find out that he'd lost most his family – including his true love.

Corbett had heard that the battle would be over soon, so he would just have to sit and wait for his father.

He entered the sorcerer's chamber and looked around. The room was dark with only one high, shuttered window. Light from outside shone in through the crack. Orrick grabbed a long stick and pulled open the shutters, flooding the room in sunshine.

"Have a seat," he told Corbett, pointing to a single rickety, old, wooden chair next to a small, round table. It seemed as if, mayhap, the sorcerer had whittled the furniture himself. There was a large bed surrounded by burgundy velvet curtains hanging from iron rods. Against the wall were several chests, and scattered around the room were candles, books, and jars filled with things he couldn't identify. The shelves were filled with dried animal skins and baskets of feathers, turtle shells, and colored stones. A dust-covered stuffed owl as well as a raven seemed to watch his every move from high above.

"Aren't owls and ravens bad omens?" asked Corbett, sitting carefully on the edge of the chair.

"Not at all," said Orrick with a chuckle. "Actually, those were my pets at one time."

"They were?" Corbett swallowed deeply thinking it odd to stuff a dead pet and put it on a shelf.

"When they were alive, I was able to communicate with them by thought alone."

"How is that possible?" asked Corbett.

"Anything is possible as long as you believe. I'm working on a spell that will allow me to shapeshift if all goes as planned."

Corbett was starting to think the old sorcerer was crazy. He was also starting to lose belief in anything after the hand life had just dealt him. There was only Corbett and his father now. Corbett wanted more than anything to run to him and fall into his arms and have his father tell him everything would be all right. As much as he wanted to believe this, there was a nagging feeling in his gut that things were only going to get worse.

"Look at this," said the sorcerer, collecting something from inside a dusty, little wooden box and cupping it in his palm. He walked over and laid it on the table in front of Corbett.

"What is it?" Corbett surveyed a round, metal piece somewhat like a coin. It looked plain and there was nothing special about it.

"It is an amulet. I've enchanted it with magic. I've seen that the baron's first-born will be in danger until the time of marriage. So this amulet will ensure the child's safety."

"It's just a plain, hammered piece of metal," he said with a shrug of his shoulders.

"Nay, it's so much more than that. Take a closer look, Corbett. This time, look *into* the amulet instead of at it."

Corbett had no idea what the addled old man meant, but he picked it up anyway. He needed a distraction to take his mind off his troubles. He tried to look into the piece, but saw nothing special. "It's still just an old piece of metal." Corbett set it back down on the table. Orrick picked it up and placed it in Corbett's palm and closed his fingers around it.

"Believe it, this time, boy. You'll see the magic in it, but only if you truly believe."

"I believe," said Corbett, but he really didn't really mean it.

"Say it again and this time close your eyes," Orrick instructed. "Feel the magic within it."

Corbett took a deep breath and released it through his mouth. He tried to clear his mind and do as the sorcerer instructed.

"Now, open your eyes," said the old man, taking his hand away at the same time.

Corbett opened his eyes slowly, then unwrapped his fingers from around the amulet and looked down to it in surprise. His mouth opened wide as well as his eyes when he saw a dragon – the baron's crest – etched upon the metal. It seemed to be glowing.

"Now do you believe in magic?" asked Orrick with a smile.

"I . . . I'm not sure," he said, still having doubt. As soon as he said the words, the dragon disappeared.

"We'll have to work on it." Orrick helped Corbett to his feet. "Right now, I need you to take this to the baroness' chamber, as she's about to give birth. Tell her she needs to give this to the baby."

"What?" asked Corbett as the sorcerer all but dragged him to the door. He didn't like the baroness and tried to always avoid her. "Why me?"

"Because it is the first step in your training. Besides, I have other things to do. I need to consult my crystal again. I've seen a prophecy involving the baron's heir."

"What prophecy?" asked Corbett curiously.

"It's a secret, Corbett. You can't tell anyone."

"I won't," said Corbett, anxious to hear the information.

"I do believe that the baron's true heir will be known by the mark of the dagger on the back of the baby's neck."

"That's it?" asked Corbett, feeling let down, expecting to hear something more. "Why is that a secret when everyone will see it anyway? I don't understand."

"I don't know yet," said Orrick. "Something is not right and I need to find out what it is. Now, I'll show you where to go and you deliver this as instructed."

CHAPTER 4

*C*orbett ran back to the sorcerer's tower as fast as his little legs would carry him. He didn't stop until he'd entered the room and slammed the door behind him.

Delivering the amulet to the baroness was the worst thing he'd ever done in his life. The woman scared him, and their encounter hadn't gone well at all. Now, to make matters worse, there was a dead midwife at the bottom of the steps and he wasn't at all sure that she hadn't been murdered.

"The baroness told me she tripped and fell," Corbett spoke aloud to himself, pacing the room and trying to believe it. Nay, something was wrong. He needed to talk to Orrick. Where was Orrick when he needed him?

The door to the tower room opened and a soldier

walked in with something wrapped up in a blanket and resting in the crook of his arm. The man looked dirty, scraped and bruised, and full of dried blood. Corbett recognized him immediately as one of the men who went to battle with his father and the baron.

"Where is the sorcerer?" asked the man in a low voice.

"He's not here," said Corbett. "Is the battle over?"

"Are you Corbett, son of Lord Evan Blake?" The man carried the object over to the table.

"I am," said Corbett, feeling that knot in his stomach again. He didn't need to be gifted to know this man brought bad news.

"Aye, the battle is over," he told him.

"Then my father and the baron have returned?" Corbett's heart about beat out of his chest as he waited for the man's answer.

"Nay. The baron has gone to Steepleton to take your father back to Blake Castle."

"Take my father? What do you mean? Is he wounded?"

"I'm sorry, Corbett, but your father is dead. He died protecting the baron."

"Nay! I don't believe you," he shouted, feeling his world crashing down around him.

"Then mayhap this will make you believe." The

soldier dropped the package he was holding onto the table and motioned to it with his head. "Go ahead, open it. It was your father's dying wish that you have it."

Corbett was in denial. He felt like crying, but he had no more tears left to shed since he'd used them all when he'd learned of the death of his mother and the disappearance of his siblings. He reached out with one shaking hand and took hold of the bloodied blanket. "I believe," he whispered, hoping for magic to bring his father back to life. Corbett wanted nothing more than to wake up and find out this was all naught but a bad dream. He pulled back the blanket slowly, and there he saw his father's sword with the four etched rings engraved in the metal. One ring for each of his children, his father had told him.

"So, he really is dead," Corbett said softly, stroking the etchings of the rings on the sword. "My mother is dead and possibly my siblings as well. Now Orrick has disappeared, too. I'm all alone now." Emotions welled in Corbett's chest. He had lost everyone and everything that he'd ever loved. How could he go on without them?

"The baron told me to watch over you until he returns," said the soldier. "He said to tell you he will foster you now, and raise you as if you were his own son because he owes it to your father. If your father hadn't taken the killing blow, the baron would be dead right now instead."

Hearing this was just too much for Corbett to bear. His legs gave out and he fell upon his father's sword, hugging it to his body. His tears came once again and fell upon the etched rings. When his tears hit the metal, he swore he saw the rings glow.

This sword was all he had left to remember his family by now. He would guard it with his life. If he believed, just like Orrick had told him, magic would happen. Mayhap, if he believed hard enough, something good would possibly come of this whole situation. After all, his father had once told him that everything happened for a reason.

But then he realized that magic was naught more than wishful thinking. He held no hope for anything anymore. Nor did he believe in wishes. He was angry with God for claiming the lives of his parents and taking his siblings away from him, too. He was also angry with Orrick for leaving him at such a crucial time.

His father had everything stripped from him because he'd married for love instead of alliance. The love of his family had Corbett's heart aching like a dagger to his chest right now. This was all wrong. Love is what caused these hardships, so Corbett closed his heart off to love on this day. Love would never bring him anything but pain and sorrow.

He ran his fingertips over the four rings etched upon the metal, feeling warmth against his skin. This was his sword now. His late father's sword would be with him forever, as it was his future as well as his past.

Corbett decided he would never be a sorcerer's apprentice. Nay, he would learn to be a warrior just like his father and his grandfather before him. He'd follow in their footsteps, and not end up worthless like his Uncle Ruford who was naught but a monk in the monastery. Corbett vowed to himself to do everything in his power to clear the sullied Blake name and bring honor back to his family even if it took him a lifetime to accomplish.

Yes, this sword was his family now. It symbolized everyone he'd ever loved and lost. He would take it with him to his grave, as this sword had once been his grandfather's, and then his father's. Now it was his. It was the symbol of his parents as well as his siblings that he would never forget. As time went on and his memories faded of those he'd loved, he'd always be reminded of them just by looking at this sword. Yes, this sword was more than just a weapon to him. It was his life now. Corbett's memories of his family would live on forever through the *Legacy of the Blade*.

FROM THE AUTHOR

As in the prequel to my *Daughters of the Dagger Series*, I must say I am sorry for the sad ending, but this is only part of the backstory that makes up the hardened character of Corbett Blake in *Lord of the Blade – Book 1* of the *Legacy of the Blade Series*. Corbett has given up on love, and he's also determined to bring back honor to the family name. When he meets Devon, a girl from his dreams that he makes his servant, everything he believes in is tested. The more he fights these repressed feelings, the stronger they become. (You can read more about his encounter with the baroness and the amulet in Book 1.)

As you continue to read the series, you will meet not only Corbett as an adult, but each of his siblings as well. The omens, you will see were correct, as his sister,

Wren, turns out to be a leader of a band of women rene-gades – and blind in *Lady Renegade – Book 2*. The twins, Madoc and Echo end up surviving and being raised as a thief and a pirate in *Lord of Illusion – Book 3*, and *Lady of the Mist – Book 4*.

If you enjoyed the prequel, please take a moment and leave me a review.

Thank you,

Elizabeth Rose

Lord of the Blade

Legacy of the Blade Series - Book 1

"Hellfire and damnation, what is going on?" The room went suddenly silent at the sound of a low bellowing voice from the other end of the hall. The servants, with their eating knives in hand, jumped to the floor and pulled the young boy along with them.

Devon didn't need to look to know that voice. It was a voice she hadn't heard since the day they'd had a visitor at the monastery.

Lord Corbett Blake stood silhouetted in the open doorway, bright sun streaking in around him. His raven watched intently from atop his shoulder. His squire rushed in behind him carrying something in his arms.

No one dared breathe, let alone give an answer to the lord's question. The raven's cry split the air.

"I leave for a few days, and upon my return I'm greeted by the merrymaking of my servants when they should be tending to their chores?" asked Corbett.

He stepped forward, the crowd parting like the Red Sea as he made his way toward the table. His squire trailed behind him struggling with what looked like a helm and a huge shield.

"Get down from there at once," Corbett demanded. Devon froze. She wasn't accustomed to jumping on command, and found herself questioning what action she should take.

"Look at me when I speak to you," said Corbett.

If only she could do as he asked, but the man was much too handsome and she was sure her face would color. Never before had she been so close to a noble. The idea thrilled her, yet frightened her at the same time.

Lord Corbett's stone face turned to the servants, and he spoke in a low tone.

"I'd suggest you all get back to work, unless you're waiting for me to live up to my horrid reputation and hand out the punishments you truly deserve."

The room cleared faster than a bread basket at the hands of hungry soldiers. When Lord Corbett turned to give his squire an order, she decided to quit the room as well. Devon took a step toward the edge of the trestle table, but his voice halted her action.

"Not you! Stay here, as I would have a word with you."

The squire opened the door to leave, causing a bright beacon of sun to shine directly on her. She was blinded momentarily, and when the door squeaked closed and the beam of light subsided, Corbett was gone.

"Looking for me?" he asked.

Her head snapped around at hearing his deep voice and her hand flew to her chest to still her heartbeat. Corbett sat on a wooden chair behind the dais, tilting back on two of its legs as he crossed his feet atop the board that served as a table. His blue eyes pierced the distance between them. One glance at his mesmerizing eyes and her body burned from within. Sensuality painted his face, though he most likely was not aware of the essence of manly beauty that encompassed his entire being.

Devon found herself fantasizing that he was lounging back upon a bed, beckoning her to his side. She wondered how it would feel to press her lips against his, or how his battle-scarred hands would feel caressing her body. Devon chastised herself for her foolish thoughts, looking down to his raven hopping around the table pecking at leftover crumbs. She was unable to face him, and unable to turn away.

He pulled off his leather gauntlets one finger at a time, as if teasing her by undressing, and threw them down with a snap upon the table. She felt her cheeks burning and knew her face was reddening, giving away her thoughts. Now, she wished that she had left the room with the others.

"Who are you? I don't recall seeing your face around here. And as servants are scarce at the moment, I'm sure I know every one." He picked up a pitcher of ale and poured some into a used wooden goblet. "Did Brother Ruford bring you here from the village?"

It was all she could do to shake her head.

His feet scraped across the table, and he slowly rested them on the floor, his eyes never leaving her. Picking up the goblet, he chugged down its contents in three gulps and then banged it down on the table. "Why don't you answer me?"

Startled by his action and intimidated by his tone, it was her own stubbornness that made her stay silent. So this was the man who ruled with an iron fist. Here was the man who had the servants running in fear every time he neared. She stared at her feet and bit her lip. She feared him, too, but for a very different reason.

Corbett slowly got to his feet and ran a finger over

the back of his raven's head before he made his way around the table and stopped directly in front of her.

"You're the girl from the monastery, aren't you?"

She nodded slightly and silently.

"Ah, then that explains it." He paced back and forth, his hand upon his chin in thought. "You, too, observe the monks' vows of silence."

Corbett watched as a surprised look came over the girl's face. He knew from the moment he walked into the hall that she had a voice. And it was a lovely one, at that. How could a brash woman such as this remain silent? She obviously only did it to challenge or anger him.

If the other servants started acting like this one, he'd soon have a problem on his hands. He'd have to teach her a lesson. It would have to be a lesson that was sure to make her speak, and stop her silly games of denying to carry out his orders. Placing his hands on the edge of the table, he lifted the board slightly, causing the trenchers and goblets to go rolling to the floor. Several hounds darted in to lick up the remains among the rushes.

The girl's eyes grew wide and she dropped the knife she was holding, but still she didn't speak. She wouldn't look at him, and this disturbed as well as intrigued him. Was she so bold as to show disrespect to her lord? Who was she? Could she be the emerald-eyed beauty from his dreams?

The table was heavy and usually took half a dozen men to move it. It strained his own muscles, but he wouldn't show weakness in front of a woman. Corbett lifted it a bit higher, expecting her to tumble off, but her balance was impeccable. No one could remain upright at such an odd angle, yet she challenged him by refusing to fall.

"God's eyes, you're a stubborn wench!" He let the table slip from his hands, banging back down with force upon the wooden frames that held it. The girl stumbled from the sudden momentum, and fell forward right toward him. He put his hands up to block himself, but somehow ended up with her in his arms.

Her arms went around his neck, and rather it be purposely or just to stop her fall, he felt himself pleased by her action. Her face brushed his accidentally, and he reveled in the silken softness of her skin. Long, unbound, mahogany hair fell around his arms halfway to the floor. It was clean, shiny hair that smelled of mint, unlike the dirty lice-infested hair of half his servants.

The warmth of her body caressed him right through his surcoat and cloak. He felt an irresistible urge to throw down his cloak upon the rushes and himself atop the girl. Entranced by her beauty, he suddenly needed to know the color of her eyes. He shifted, and felt her body tense. With one finger, he tilted her chin upward, but could only see her closed lids.

"Open your eyes, Wench. You look like you're longing to be kissed."

Her eyes shot open at his comment, and she struggled to free herself of his hold. He released her out of courtesy, not out of want, and nodded his head.

"Green. I thought so."

Lord of the Blade

Lady Renegade

Legacy of the Blade Series - Book 2

Prologue

Scotland, 1343

"Keep that bairned bitch of yers quiet, Storm." Chieftain Ian MacKeefe's hoarse whisper came through gritted teeth.

Storm MacKeefe knew his father was looking for a fight, and the small band of English soldiers heading straight for them was his target.

"Da, she's only tryin' to protect us." Storm ran his hand over the Scottish Deerhound's matted fur. Immediately, the hound stopped growling. Noticing the bright moonbeams streaking across the dog's head, he pulled her back into the shadows of the thatched Highland cottage they were using for cover.

"She'll be no guid to us until after the pups are born," snapped the chieftain, eyeing the dog's large stomach. "She's going to alert those English bastards that we're here."

Storm didn't respond. He only clenched his jaw and nodded to his father who was sitting majestically high upon his steed. As usual, he didn't agree with the man, but decided this wasn't the time for a confrontation. For twenty years, he followed his domineering father loyally, not daring to defy the man's word in public as he tried to live up to what was expected of a chieftain's son.

But tonight, something was different. Though the breeze was fairly warm, he felt a shiver run the length of his spine. A mist swirled around his ankles as the night rolled in, the air hanging heavy around him. He didn't understand his own apprehension, but a feeling deep inside warned him he should have left his pregnant hound back at camp with the women and children of the clan.

Hoofbeats and wagon wheels crashed over rocky terrain, and slowed almost to a stop as the English soldiers approached the cottage.

"Get ready to attack," whispered Ian MacKeefe, raising his hand above his head to gain the full attention of his silent warriors. Then in a low mumble he said, "Let's show these English curs no mercy for passin' over MacKeefe lands."

"Da, nay!" Storm held the reins of his horse in one hand, as he reached up to grab his father's idle wrist.

Ian's eyes darted to Storm's grip before slowly making a path to his face. Storm released his hold, startled at the unspoken pain now burning in his father's eyes. Ian's craggy brows dipped in frustration as he shook his head slowly.

"Ye just dinna understand, Son, do ye?"

"Nay," answered Storm. "I dinna understand why ye always choose battle over peace."

Storm felt his father's disapproval raining down on him like hellfire from the sky. The chieftain's penetrating gaze seemed to burn a hole clear through to his very soul.

"Mount yer horse, Son. And dinna try to stop me again, for I thought I've raised ye better than to question my word," warned his father.

The Deerhound growled once again at the English soldiers, and Storm found himself thinking that even this docile dog by nature had grown to be a killer. He never wanted to train the dog to kill anything but deer and small game to help feed the clan, but he found himself doing it anyway to please his father.

Storm looked down at his pregnant hound, feeling a raw grief settling in his stomach. His hound was faithful and would do anything for him, even kill a man if ordered. He could only hope this night wouldn't lead to that.

Lady Renegade

Lord of Illusion

Legacy of the Blade Series - Book 3

She rode her steed hard through the woods, branches scratching her skin and tearing at her traveling clothes. Still, she didn't care. One glance over her shoulder told her she was yet to be followed. But when she looked a second time, a rider on horseback approached her, gaining on her quickly. In her carelessness, she misdirected her horse and it reared up, causing her to fall from her sidesaddle to the hard ground below. The rider came up behind her and she felt two strong arms pull her to her feet.

"Nay!" she shouted, pushing him away, "I won't go with you to marry that ogre."

Then she realized he wasn't a guard at all, but rather the old man in the road who'd robbed them.

"Let go of me," she cried. In her struggles, the man's hood slipped from his head. Though he had a beard and eyebrows of nearly white, the hair on his head was dark as a starless night.

"Hold still," the man ground out. A young man's voice slipped from his lips instead of the old, crackly voice she'd heard on the road.

"You are not an old man at all," she spat. "You are an imposter. Who are you?"

Madoc ap Powell looked at the beautiful woman before him who was demanding his name as if he would really tell her.

"Who are *you*?" he asked in return.

"I am Lady Abigail of Blackmore," she retorted. "And I demand you release me."

"You, my lady, are the one who alerted the guards to my actions and almost got me killed." She was a feisty wench, he'd give her that. And twice as observant as any of the guards.

"They *will* kill you," she said. "Just as soon as they follow – which will be at any moment now."

"Nay, my lady. That is where you are wrong. For, at this moment, they are fighting off bandits who are headed in the opposite direction. I sincerely doubt they've even noticed you are missing."

"So you set up an attack and now you come for me?"

"I had naught to do with the attack. I work on my own. I just happened upon the opportunity before they did, that's all."

"Work?" she mimicked the word he'd used. "Hah. I sincerely doubt you have ever worked an honest job or day in your life. And to set things straight, I do not like to be referred to as an opportunity."

Once again, she was very observant, although he *had* worked at an honest job for a few years of his life. But he'd seen where honest work had gotten him when he'd ended up in the dungeon. Nay, what he did now was the better of the choices, and also what his mother had taught him to do from childhood.

He took a sheep bladder filled with water from his side and splashed it upon his face to rid himself of his disguise. The white powder in his beard and mustache washed out, leaving it as dark as the hair on his head. The powder in his eyebrows followed. He gave a sharp intake of breath at the coldness on his skin, then took a swig of the water and offered her some.

"Nay," she said, turning her head. As she tried to walk away, he realized her gown had caught on a branch.

"Well, Lady Abigail, I see your escape is foiled. You

are caught not only by me but also by the guardians of nature."

"I wasn't trying to escape!" she exclaimed.

When she looked back up to him, he perused her beauty. A few years younger than he, she seemed to be, mayhap, one and twenty summers. Her hair was golden silk, spun from the faeries of the forest themselves. Her eyes were blue – deep blue – and clear like that of a midsummer's night sky. And her skin was alabaster and looked soft and supple.

"Well, I am glad to hear you were not trying to escape," he told her. "Because then you'll be willing to come with me when I return you for a reward."

Lord of Illusion

Lady of the Mist

Legacy of the Blade Series Book - 4

Garrett made his way to the forecastle and climbed the raised platform as they approached the other ship. Sure enough, black sails. This was the pirate ship he'd been searching for. What a discovery to finally find it.

The wind picked up from the approaching storm, filling the single square sail of the cog. The clinker-built hull had high sides that served as good protection from marauders of the sea. However, this was a merchant ship. The flat bottom was designed for loading and unloading cargo in shallow ports. It wasn't designed for rough seas and could very well capsize in a strong wind.

The ship held one hundred tuns in the hold. Today,

they were traveling light, at only half its capacity. This made him nervous. Garrett eyed the dark, roiling sky overhead. He knew what he had to do but, still, the crew's safety concerned him.

"Archers, get in position," he cried. "Silas, take her in close. I am going to board off the forecastle. Get the grappling hooks and ropes ready," he called over his shoulder as they came up alongside the ship.

"Aye, Captain," said Silas.

Garrett saw the crew of his target ship rushing around, looking very disorganized. He would be able to use this to his advantage. But the man in the lookout could have a weapon to throw or something to drop on him. He looked up and aimed his crossbow. He couldn't allow himself to be a sitting target from the man up above. He pulled back the windlass and lined up his bolt for the shot.

Echo quickly replaced her cap, tucking her hair back underneath. She would never be able to fight with her hair in her eyes now that the wind had picked up tremendously. Skye and the male osprey flew in circles just above the ship. They wanted to land in the nest to get out of the storm.

Glancing down to the deck, she saw her father and the crew running around aimlessly, trying to prepare for the battle about to take place. If they hadn't been soused, they would have already been boarding and attacking the Cinque Ports ship.

"Hard ta starboard," shouted her father, giving the sternsman the order to turn the ship. The *Seahawk* bounced and leaned in the high waves that the storm now brought upon them. A gale of wind hit Echo head on, nearly knocking her from the basket. "Go ta half-sail," shouted her father, but that was going to be impossible now that they had to concentrate on the attack. The cold, sharp rain sliced down upon her like arrows from an archer's bow.

Then she spied a man aboard the Cinque Ports ship upon the forecastle and he aimed his crossbow right at her! She barely had time to dodge out of the way of his bolt, The ship jerked and she had to grab on to the pole in the center of the basket in order not to be thrown out.

The sickening shriek of a bird brought her attention upward. The man's bolt had lodged into one of the hawks, taking it down into the sea.

"Nay!" she cried, not knowing if it was Skye or the male hawk that just went to its death at the hands of her attackers. The ship leaned once again and the sound of creaking wood and slapping ropes filled the air. The two eggs rolled out of the nest and through the slats in the basket and over the side. She watched in horror as they plummeted down to the deck far below. "Damnation and hell-fire," she shouted, first looking to the path the eggs had taken, and then back to the passenger from the Cinque Ports ship who was jumping from his fighting post by means of the bowsprit. He foolishly boarded their ship even before his crew tossed the grappling lines.

"Attack!" shouted her father from below her. The crew of the *Seahawk* picked up long, wooden poles with spikes and axes. Shouting, they rushed toward the side of the ship. The Cinque Ports men were just throwing their grappling hooks aboard, but nature took its course. One more huge gust of wind changed the outcome for everyone.

Garrett watched in disbelief as the wind hit their single square sail head on and sent his ship backwards away from the vessel he now stood upon. His archers opened fire from the castle decks, but the strong winds sent their arrows askew. While several landed on deck, not a one hit its mark.

He feared for his men in the storm. And now he feared for his own life as well. He stood alone against a band of cutthroats that would most likely kill him before they had food to break their fast.

"Damn!" The ships separated so quickly in the storm that there would be no retribution for these pirates now. He could only hope Silas would direct the ship for Great Yarmouth as he'd instructed, and not be capsized in the storm.

Garrett turned and raised his crossbow as two of the pirate crew rushed him. He managed to loose one bolt. It grazed the shoulder of the first man who cried out. But Garrett's weapon was too bulky and the windlass too slow to load quickly. He threw it down and grabbed his sword from his side instead. Before he even had a chance to use it, someone from up in the rigging dropped atop him, knocking him to the ground.

"Ye killed my bird!" came a high voice in his ear.

Garrett's sword was knocked out of his hand from the impact. He hurriedly reached for the dagger attached to his waist belt. The attacker's small hand reached out in a strong grip, digging his nails into Garrett's wrist, trying to make him release it. The edge of the man's sword rested against his throat as the rest of the rowdy crew came forward and urged the man on.

"Aye, let's see ye spear 'im," called out one man.

"Kill 'im," shouted another. Then the pirates started laughing.

Garrett managed to disarm the man. As the ship tossed in the waves, their bodies rolled together over the deck only to be stopped by the planking of the ship's wall.

He didn't understand why none of the rest of the men stepped in to seize him. Instead, they found it amusing to watch him and this young man struggle. Garrett managed to pin his attacker to the ground. He held his dagger to the man's throat. The pirates behind him laughed and shouted out obscenities in the pouring rain. Water dripped off his long hair and hit the pinned man in the eyes.

"Devil take ye, ye landlubber king's bitch!

The men's laughter roared from behind him. Garrett thought he understood why. This man's voice was high and his body small. If Garrett's instincts served him correctly, he'd been fooled. He yanked off the man's cap and watched as ebony tresses spilled around his captor's head. As he looked closer at the man's face through the dirt and grime, he realized this was not a man at all, but a woman!

Lady of the Mist

ABOUT ELIZABETH

Elizabeth Rose is a multi-published, bestselling author, writing medieval, historical, contemporary, paranormal, and western romance. Her books are available as EBooks, paperbacks, and audiobooks as well.

Her favorite characters in her works include dark, dangerous and tortured heroes, and feisty, independent heroines who know how to wield a sword. She loves writing 14th century medieval novels, and is well-known for her many series.

Her twelve-book small town contemporary series, Tarnished Saints, was inspired by incidents in her own life.

After being traditionally published, she started self-publishing, creating her own covers and book trailers on a dare from her two sons.

Elizabeth loves the outdoors. In the summertime, you can find her in her secret garden with her laptop, swinging in her hammock working on her next book. Elizabeth is a born storyteller and passionate about sharing her works with her readers.

Please visit her website at **Elizabethrosenovels.com** to read excerpts from any of her novels and get sneak peeks at covers of upcoming books. You can follow her on **Twitter, Facebook, Goodreads** or **BookBub.** Be sure to sign up for her **newsletter** so you don't miss out on new releases or upcoming events.

ALSO BY ELIZABETH ROSE

Medieval

Legendary Bastards of the Crown Series

Seasons of Fortitude Series

Secrets of the Heart Series

Legacy of the Blade Series

Daughters of the Dagger Series

MadMan MacKeefe Series

Barons of the Cinque Ports Series

Second in Command Series

Holiday Knights Series

Highland Chronicles Series

Medieval/Paranormal

Elemental Magick Series

Greek Myth Fantasy Series

Tangled Tales Series

Contemporary

Tarnished Saints Series

Working Man Series

Western

Cowboys of the Old West Series

And more!

Please visit http://elizabethrosenovels.com

Elizabeth Rose

Made in the USA
Middletown, DE
02 December 2020

25933191R00040